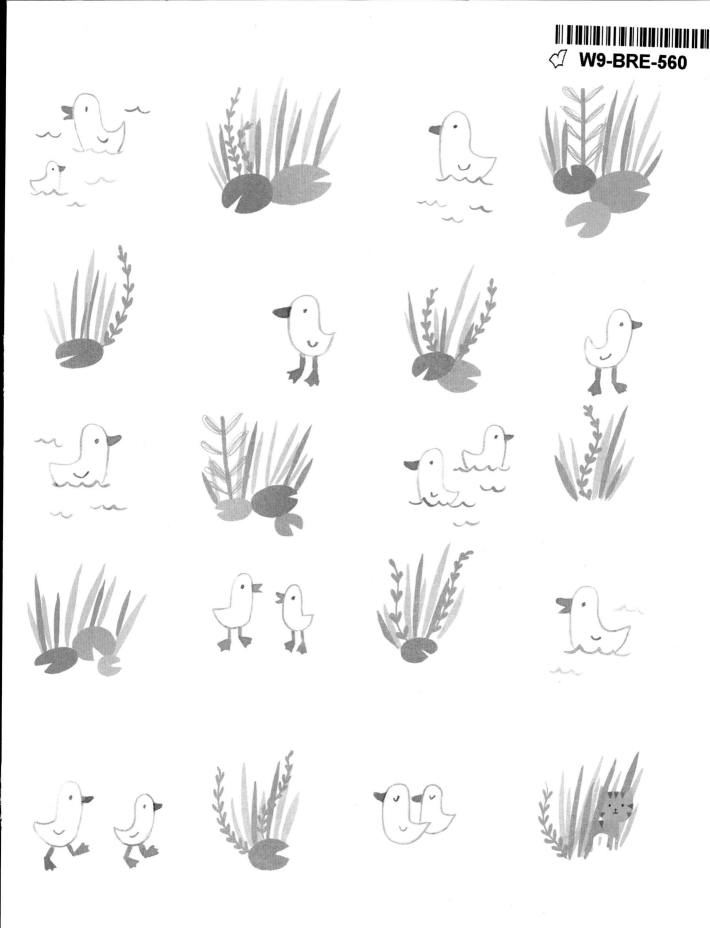

QUACKERS

LIZ WONG

ALFRED A. KNOPF 🐕 NEW YORK

For my family, a whole flock of odd ducks

THIS IS A BORZOI BOOK PUBLISHED BY ALFRED A. KNOPF

Copyright © 2016 by Liz Wong

All rights reserved. Published in the United States by Alfred A. Knopf,

an imprint of Random House Children's Books, a division of Penguin Random House LLC, New York.

Knopf, Borzoi Books, and the colophon are registered trademarks of Penguin Random House LLC.

Visit us on the Web! randomhousekids.com

Educators and librarians, for a variety of teaching tools, visit us at RHTeachersLibrarians.com

Library of Congress Cataloging-in-Publication Data is available upon request.

ISBN 978-0-553-51154-3 (trade) — ISBN 978-0-553-51155-0 (lib. bdg.) — ISBN 978-0-553-51156-7 (ebook)

The illustrations in this book were created digitally and with watercolor.

MANUFACTURED IN MALAYSIA

March 2016

10 9 8 7 6 5 4 3 2

First Edition

Quackers is
a duck.

He knows he is a duck
because he lives at the duck pond
with all the other ducks.

And everyone he knows
is a duck.

duck

duck

duck

duck

duck

duck

duck

duck

He often has trouble communicating.

He doesn't care much for the dinner options.

slugs

snails

seeds

worms

algae

duckweed

Not duckweed again!

Most of all,
he hates getting wet.

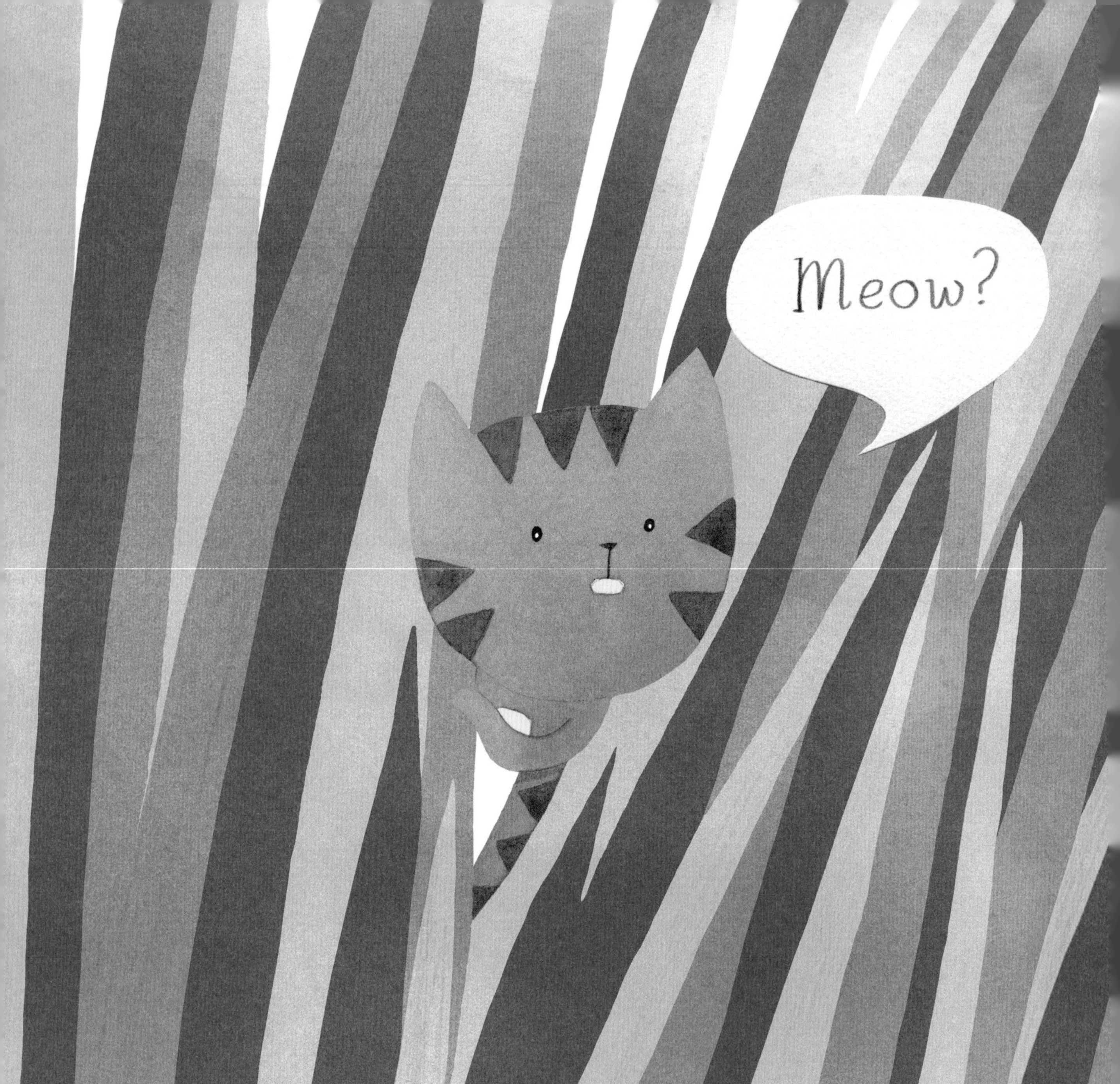

Then one day, Quackers met a strange duck.

Quackers was overjoyed.

The strange duck, whose name turned out to be Mittens, seemed to find something very amusing.

Ha ha ha! He thinks he's a duck!

Mittens thought for a moment and said:
You'd better come with me.

Quackers had never been anywhere so entirely unlike home.

Inside was a whole *flock* of strange ducks.
Ducks just like Quackers.

Just look at all those ducks!

We're cats, silly!

We chase mice,

drink milk,

and clean ourselves.

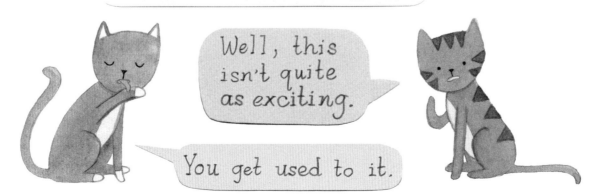

Before long, Quackers
felt right at home.

Quackers liked being a cat,
but he began to miss
the duck pond.

He missed the rustle
of the wind through
the reeds.

He missed snuggling under a warm, feathery wing.

purrrrrrrrrr

He even missed the taste of duckweed.

This isn't so bad!

And when he arrived
back at the pond,

he realized that,
most of all,
he missed his friends.

Now Quackers spends part of his days at the farm...

chasing mice,

drinking milk,

and cleaning himself.

Quackers is a duck.

And Quackers is a cat.

But, most of all, he's just Quackers, and that makes him completely happy.